Digging Up the Truth

How Do I Love Others
the Way God Loves Them?

KAYLA OLMSTEAD

ISBN 978-1-63874-016-2 (paperback)
ISBN 978-1-63874-017-9 (digital)

Christian Faith Publishing, Inc.
832 Park Avenue
Meadville, PA 16335
www.christianfaithpublishing.com

Printed in the United States of America

Be kind to one another, tenderhearted, forgiving one another, as God in Christ forgave you.

—Ephesians 4:32

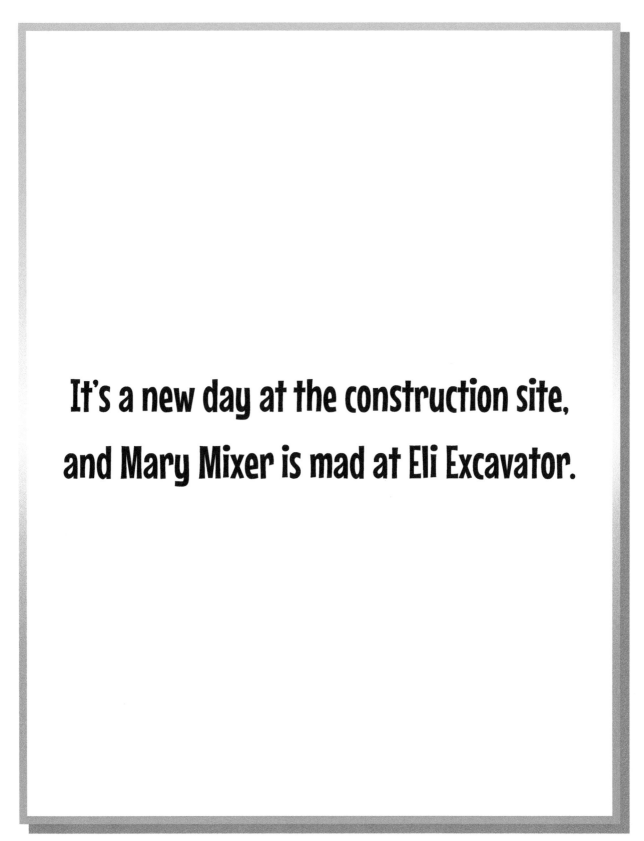

It's a new day at the construction site, and Mary Mixer is mad at Eli Excavator.

Eli was being mean to Mary. He wouldn't let her play with him or help her set up the new swing set.

Mary was so mad she started calling Eli names.

Benjamin Bulldozer did not like seeing his friends being mean to each other. He reminded them that God wants us to love others.

9

Loving others means being kind
and not calling others names.

If someone is being mean,
God wants us to forgive them
even if they aren't sorry.

Eli was sad he had been mean to Mary. He apologized to her and helped her with the new swing set.

Mary was sorry she didn't forgive Eli and had started calling him names. She apologized too, and the three friends played together for the rest of the day.

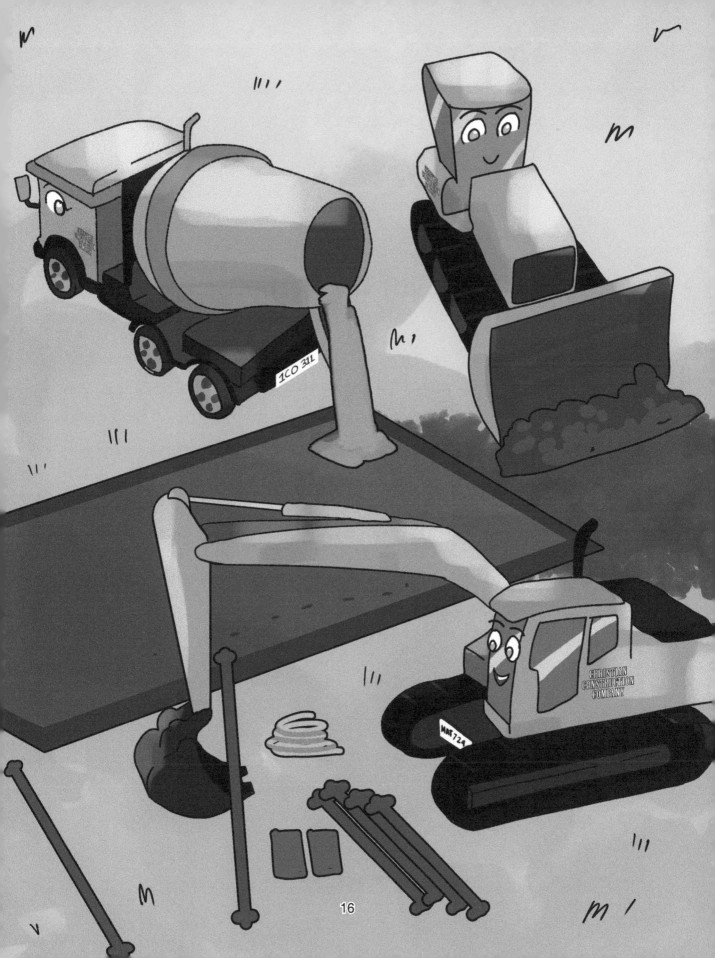

About the Author

Kayla is a stay-at-home mom to three boys. Her oldest son loves all things vehicles, which helped inspire the characters for the book. As a mom and a Christian, she wants to help children construct a solid foundation on which to build their relationship with God. Just as in life, it takes a little digging to begin building! A Texas native and a graduate of Lubbock Christian University, she and her family live in North Dakota.